ONE DAY IN SUMMER

For all the family
in the house at Briar Neck

One Day in Summer

by JEAN VAN LEEUWEN
drawings by RICHARD FISH

Random House · New York

O. P.

A piece of sun came into the room
and landed on my bed.
I opened one eye and saw
a white lace canopy high above me.
I opened one ear and heard
the waves coming and going and coming back again.
I took a deep breath and smelled
a funny salty smell.
And then I knew
I was in the big bed in the front room
at Grandfather's house
by the sea.

After breakfast
on the way to the beach
where the tickly grass grows tall
I found a grasshopper.

I kept it in my hand
not squeezing
just saving to put in a jar
and when I opened my hand
just checking
making sure it was breathing
it hopped away.

Steps made of rock go down to the beach
but I climbed down the cliff.
There are places the right size for fingers and toes
if you know just where to look.
Find a ledge here
slide down the smooth side to the flat rock
then jump
into soft, warm, welcoming sand.

There was no one on the beach but me
and a little bird playing a game
on the dark sand near the sea.
His feet made crisscrosses
feathery light
as he raced each wave to shore.
I tried to catch him but he was gone.
Why wouldn't he play the game with me?

A girl came walking up the beach
picking up things the tide left behind
when it went out.
She had a necklace made of seaweed,
four white pebbles, and a piece of green glass
worn by the sea.

I dug my toes into the wet sand
and found a sand dollar,
round and pink with a flower on it.
"Look," I said and put it in her hand.
She smiled.
And then I looked up and saw Grandfather
climbing down the stone steps.
"Come," I said
and we ran to meet him.

We built castles by the water's edge
scooping out a moat and
piling the wet, crumbly sand
into towers, windows, walls
with a feather on top for a flag.
Mine was biggest (Grandfather helped)
strong enough for any attack
and then a big wave came
and washed it away.

The sun was sitting on top of the sky
when Grandmother rang the bell.
We dropped our pails and shovels
and had a race
to the orange umbrella with the green stripes.
The picnic basket was full of sandwiches
wrapped up in little bags
so no sand could get in.
I took mine to share with a seagull
sitting on a lifeboat
but when I got in he flew away.
I watched him fly higher and higher
until he went inside a cloud
and then I ate my crusts myself.

I took my pail and walked along
where the ocean threw the shells.
Some were broken but some were just right
white with ruffled edges
or all curled up
(someone was living in one)
or frilly or plain.
A wave set one down on the sand
then took it back
but I caught it in my hand
and thought, "Where did you come from?
Where have you been?"

I rode a wave.
Grandfather showed me how.
Way out deep where waves grow
I waited on my yellow raft
until a big one came along.
Then I paddled hard
racing to catch it
as it grew taller
and taller
then—crash!—
it broke and set me down
gently on the shore.
I rode a wave.

It was almost suppertime when
Grandfather and I took a walk
down the beach
just we two, not saying a word.

I found seaweed to dress up in,
a piece of wood from a shipwreck,
and a pebble
just as round as round.

Then the sun began to go away
as I walked in Grandfather's footsteps
up the beach
up the rock steps
through the tickly grass
to Grandfather's house.